Peg Sundberg
"Cowgirl Peg"
Oct 30, 2018

BELONGS TO:

Life is an adventure!
Climb on the saddle
and enjoy the ride!

Cowgirl Peg

In loving memory of my Mother.

She is my guardian angel

LIBRARY OF CONGRESS CATALOGING-IN-PUBLICATION DATA
Sundberg, Peggy.
Cowgirl Peg and the Great Race
p. cm.
ISBN 978-0-615-59075-2. SOFTCOVER
1. Title — Author — Cowgirl Peg. 2. Juv. Lit.
3. Dogs — pets — horses — exercise
— juvenile teamwork — character traits.
2011916981

Third edition
Shweiki, 2018
Printed in USA

PUBLISHED BY: Cowgirl Peg Enterprises
CowgirlPeg2@gmail.com
www.CowgirlPeg.com

COPYRIGHT: 2011 © Peggy Sundberg
Art by Pat Wiles
DESIGN BY: F + P Graphic Design, Inc.

Cowgirl Peg
and the
Great Race

Peggy Sundberg

Watercolors by
Pat Wiles

Cowgirl Peg

Annie

James

Shortstuff

Wise Guy

Lacey

Lonesome

Oakie

Red

Harley

Muffin

Jazmine

Cowgirl Peg lived on a horse ranch at the edge of the mountains. She often sat on her porch, enjoying the beautiful sunsets with her dogs Jazmine, Harley and Muffin. One evening while watching the horses in the pasture, she observed, "My critters are lazy and gaining weight! How did that happen? What can I do?" She thought and thought until finally, a great idea popped into her head.

"What if I sponsor a big race, creating three teams that would compete against each other? This could be exciting and fun! My animal-friends will love it! I can lead one team, but I need two helpers. I'll invite my grandchildren, Annie and James, to join me."

Since they loved visiting their grandmother's ranch, Annie and James happily agreed to be team-leaders. They packed their suitcases and grabbed their sleeping bags. "Don't forget your favorite pillow," Annie reminded James.

"Got it!" James replied. "I'm so excited! I might not be able to sleep tonight!"

"Me, either," Annie yawned. However, they crawled into their beds and fell asleep, dreaming of a great race at Grandma Peg's ranch.

The next morning, Cowgirl Peg drove Annie and James to her home. Her three dogs barked a greeting as she opened the ranch gate. After closing it, Cowgirl Peg pointed to the horses in the pasture. "Look at Shortstuff with his big tummy! He might be short, but he has eaten too many sugar cubes."

"Wise Guy, Red, Lacey and Oakie also eat too many horse cookies and treats. Instead of running around the pasture, they lazily walk."

"Now look at Lonesome,"
Cowgirl Peg continued. "Even though
he has a problem with his back leg, he exercises
daily. He eats healthy oats and carrots instead of sugar.
His hair is shiny and he looks great."

"What should we do first?" asked Annie.

"Let's plan the race and choose teams," James suggested.

Sitting around the table, they sketched a map of the ranch, marking the hills, trees and ponds. Annie studied the drawing, then suggested, "What if the race is divided into four parts? The animals can climb the hills, hike through the forest and swim across the big pond, followed by the three of us racing on bicycles."

"That's a great idea!" James agreed. "Each team has four members and the race has four sections. It's perfect!"

"Sounds good to me," Cowgirl Peg answered. "Let's gather the animals in the barn and share our plans. I think they will be as excited as we are!"

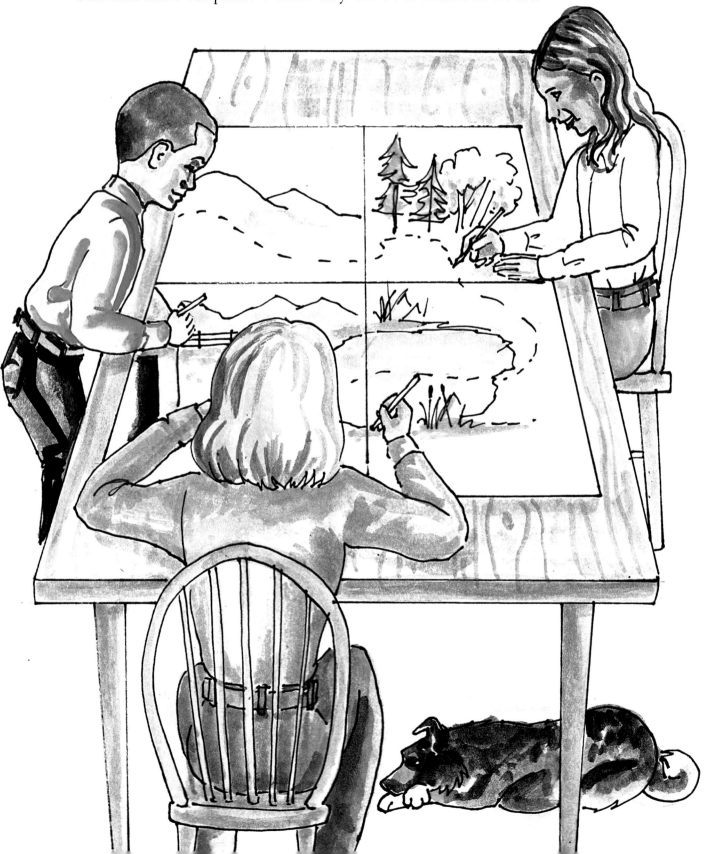

Cowgirl Peg whistled, calling the horses and dogs. One by one, they entered the barn. Muffin and Harley ran beside Wise Guy, followed by Lacey, Shortstuff, Lonesome, and Oakie.

"Uh-oh, I think Red and Jazmine are missing," stated James. "I wonder where they could be."

Annie and James searched the barn. Hearing a noise in the feed room, they peeked behind the door, discovering a red horse-tail and a tan dog-tail. With their heads buried in the sweet treat bag, Red and Jazmine had eaten so much, they looked like they might explode!

"Oh no!" exclaimed Annie. She wrapped a rope around Red's neck while James put a leash on Jazmine's collar. "Let's get them out of here!"

Cowgirl Peg laughed when she saw the two animals. "Red, was this your idea? Jazmine, you ate so many treats, you look like a balloon!"

"My friends, I have important news. When I watched each of you in the pasture last week, I saw lazy horses and dogs. Lonesome is the only one that eats well and exercises daily. We should all do the same."

"James, Annie and I have a plan. Three teams will compete to win a wonderful week at the beach. After four weeks of preparation, including lots of exercise, we'll race for the prize. We can call it *Cowgirl Peg's Great Race!*"

"Annie and James, let's draw straws and select our teams," their grandmother instructed. "I will hold three different straws in my hand. Whoever picks the smallest straw is first; the medium straw is second; the longest straw is last."

After choosing, they compared the sizes of the straws. "Woohoo! Mine is shortest!" shouted James. Annie's straw earned her second place.

"Well," Cowgirl Peg stated, "I guess I get final choices. James, you may choose your first team member".

James studied the animals. Wise Guy nodded his head in anticipation, while Shortstuff showed off by jumping in the air. The dogs barked, hoping to be chosen first. Finally, James pointed at the one quiet animal: "Lonesome, I choose you because you can teach the others about healthy exercising and eating. I know you are not able to run, but I think you can swim better and faster than the others. Welcome to my team!"

Annie chose Harley as her first member. "He is the fastest dog of all and I'm sure he will help my team win!"

Cowgirl Peg slowly looked around the circle of animals. "This is a tough decision, but I choose Jazmine as my first team-member. Jaz, you need to lose some of those pounds before the race."

Jazmine groaned. "Maybe I can eat a few dog cookies when no one is looking," she thought.

Watching her, Cowgirl Peg warned, "My furry friend, don't even think about sneaking into the sweet treats!"

The three leaders continued choosing their members, making a list.

RED Team	GREEN Team	YELLOW Team
James	**Annie**	**Cowgirl Peg**
Lonesome	Harley	Jazmine
Muffin	Red	Oakie
Shortstuff	Wise Guy	Lacey

The next morning each team met to discuss their plans. Lonesome shared his healthy exercise ideas with James, Muffin and Shortstuff. Annie asked Wise Guy to develop a training program for their team. Cowgirl Peg informed her team that they would be running laps, doing jumping jacks and pushups daily. "We will eat many fruits and vegetables from the garden. Carrots, apples and oats are much better than cookies and sugar cubes. Each day will begin and end with exercise."

Over the next four weeks, the teams ran, jumped, climbed hills, and swam in the pond. The horses pulled fresh carrots from the garden and picked sweet apples from the trees, while the dogs ate more dog food and fewer treats. Cowgirl Peg, Annie and James rode their bicycles many miles. They added lots of freshly picked vegetables to their diets and drank many glasses of milk. Their biggest challenge was eating only one chocolate chip cookie per day!

A few days before the race, the teams met to review the rules. Glancing at each member, Cowgirl Peg stated, "This is a friendly race with an honor code. Honesty and courtesy are important. You should signal the next teammate to begin by touching noses when finishing your part of the race. I trust you to do that."

Jumping in the air, Annie and James cheered "Go Team, GO!" The animal friends hopped and gave each other big "high-5's". The air was filled with excitement.

Finally, the big day arrived. Eager to begin the race, Shortstuff, Red and Lacey danced and pranced at the starting line. After following a trail over two very large hills, they would touch noses with Muffin, Wise Guy and Jazmine , who must find their way through two miles of thick forest. Next, Lonesome, Harley and Oakie would dive into the big pond, swimming for the other shore where Cowgirl Peg, James and Annie would be waiting to finish the race on their bicycles.

After sharing "good luck" wishes, Cowgirl Peg blew the starting whistle. The race was on!

Red took off in a full gallop, running like the wind towards the first hill. Shortstuff bucked as he ran, while Lacey calmly trotted away.

"Uh-oh," moaned Annie. "I forgot to warn Red that running full speed in the beginning of a long race is not smart. He's going to be really tired by the time he gets to the second hill."

"The same goes for Shortstuff if he doesn't quit bucking!" James added.

Reaching the top of the first hill, Red gasped for air. Shortstuff stopped beside him with leg cramps caused by too much bucking. With a grin on her face, Lacey calmly trotted by. Red and Shortstuff rested a few minutes, then took off once more. They sped by Lacey at the bottom of the second hill. However, Red ran slower and slower. Shortstuff stopped once more to rest his legs. Still trotting, Lacey passed by with a wave of her tail. She crossed over the hill, reaching the end of the trail where Jazmine eagerly waited for her signal to run. Red and Shortstuff slowly walked down the hill, arriving at the finish line a few minutes later. Between breaths, Red touched noses with Wise Guy. Shortstuff gave one last little buck before touching noses with Muffin.

Wise Guy stood quietly, thinking about smart choices. He decided to follow the two dogs into the forest, letting them sniff their way along the path. Jazmine led as they jumped over big logs and waded through two creeks, slowly finding their way toward the end. Suddenly all three animals stopped. A huge boulder sat on the trail! It was stuck between very thick trees on one side and a steep rock cliff on the other. Now what? Jazmine and Muffin sat down, looking at each other.

After studying the rock, Wise Guy backed into it, pushing with all 1,000 pounds of his strength. At first, the boulder just wiggled, but finally rolled forward. Wise Guy continued pushing until the trail widened. He grinned at the two dogs, then spun around and ran for the meadow by the pond. Muffin and Jazmine chased after him, but their legs were too short. Touching noses with Harley, Wise Guy cheered. Moments later, Jazmine and Muffin reached the meadow, sending Lonesome and Oakie toward the pond.

Harley dove in first, dog-paddling as fast as he could. Lonesome and Oakie charged into the water, horse-paddling after him. Surely they could swim faster than a little dog! Lonesome held his head high, swimming as he had practiced. Oakie tried to keep up, but could not. With just fifty feet remaining before the opposite shore, Lonesome passed Harley. He proudly climbed out of the pond, leaving the other two behind. His hard work earned him first place in the swim!

After touching noses with Lonesome, James jumped on his bike, pedaling as fast as he could. Harley and Oakie ran out of the pond, touching noses with Annie and Cowgirl Peg, who waited on their bikes. "James is going really fast," Annie warned. "Catching him won't be easy."

Arriving at a fork in the road, James decided to take a short cut through the field. Riding through old wagon ruts, over small rocks and sticks, he headed for the path to the finish line. Suddenly, he heard a pop. "Oh, no!" Stopping to look, he saw a very flat tire. "Now what will I do? My team is counting on me to win!"

Cowgirl Peg and Annie weren't far behind, but decided to stay on the gravel path. A few minutes later, they saw James standing by his bike. "Annie, we can keep going and leave James behind, or we can stop to help. I have an air pump. What do you think?"

Frowning, Annie replied, "I suppose we should stop and fix his tire."

While fixing the bicycle, Cowgirl Peg looked toward the finish line where her animal friends anxiously waited. "We worked very hard getting ready for this race. The two teams that don't win will be so disappointed."

Thinking for a moment, she said "I have an idea."

Cowgirl Peg whispered a plan to James and Annie. Smiling, they nodded an approval.

Pointing their bicycles toward the finish line, they rode side-by-side. Raising hands in victory, they evenly crossed the finish line. The animals stared in surprise, then laughed. They were all winners! Shortstuff bucked. Lacey flipped her tail. Wise Guy nodded. Red and Oakie danced. Lonesome whinnied. The dogs stood on their back legs, slapping paws with each other.

Hugging her two grandchildren, Cowgirl Peg exclaimed, "I guess we will all be going to the beach!"

The following week, after playing in the surf and sand, the animals met with their leaders.
Cowgirl Peg climbed onto Red's back and announced, "My friends, we should be very proud of
our accomplishments. After four weeks of exercising and choosing healthy food, we feel great."

"Let's make every day a *Great Race To Stay Fit!*"

Cowgirl Peg, Annie and James enjoying a bike ride.

Shortstuff

Helping Cowgirl Peg stack the hay

Wise Guy

Muffin gets some rest on the trail

I love to exercise! I am now in my sixties and still enjoy exercising with my horses, riding my bike, climbing mountains, hiking in the woods, swimming in the summer and snowshoeing in the winter. Adventure will always be a big part of my life.

Annie and James also enjoy being active: Annie loves to run and swim. She competes in youth triathlons, races and swim team meets. James loves to swim, bike and play kickball. He is especially good at diving into big waves at the beach.

Exercising, exploring and eating healthy foods = a fun lifestyle! Try it… you'll like it, too!

Cowgirl Peg

Red sneaks a bite of hay

Cowgirl Peg with Lonesome and Daisy

Jazmine

Harley

Cowgirl Peg with Red and Oakie

Pat Wiles, the illustrator, on her horse Lacey

Other Cowgirl Peg books

Lonesome the Little Horse
His Mountain Adventure

Based on a true story

Text by
Peggy Sundberg
Watercolor Art by
Pat Wiles

Isabelle
Lives a Dream

Text by
Peggy Sundberg
Watercolors by
Pat Wiles

Jazmine's
Incredible Story

The True Adventures
of Cowgirl Peg's
Beloved Companion

Text by
Peggy Sundberg
Watercolor Art by
Pat Wiles

Okey-Dokey Oakie

Text by
Peggy Sundberg
Watercolor Art by
Pat Wiles

Shortstuff Bucks!

Text by
Peggy Sundberg
Watercolor Art by
Pat Wiles